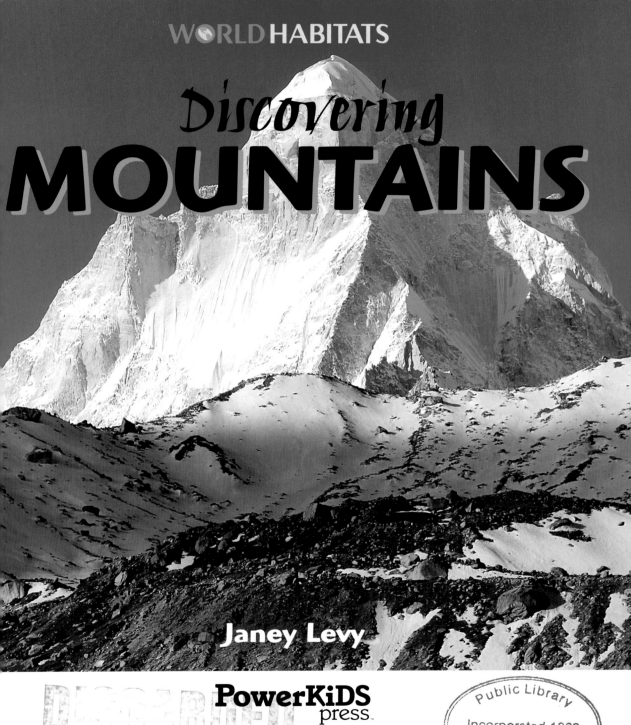

Discovering
MOUNTAINS

Janey Levy

PowerKiDS
press
New York

Published in 2008 by The Rosen Publishing Group, Inc.
29 East 21st Street, New York, NY 10010

First Edition

Editors: Geeta Sobha and Joanne Randolph
Book Design: Julio Gil
Photo Researcher: Nicole Pristash

Photo Credits: All pictures © Shutterstock.com.

Library of Congress Cataloging-in-Publication Data

Levy, Janey.
  Discovering mountains / Janey Levy. — 1st ed.
      p. cm. — (World habitats)
  Includes index.
  ISBN-13: 978-1-4042-3785-8 (library binding)
  ISBN-10: 1-4042-3785-2 (library binding)
  1. Mountain ecology—Juvenile literature. 2. Mountains—Juvenile literature.
I. Title.
  QH541.5.M65L49 2008
  577.5'3—dc22

                                                2006103369

Manufactured in Malaysia

Contents

Mountains and Their Biomes

A mountain is a high land mass made up of more than one biome. A biome is a community of plants and animals that live together in a region and depend on each other. Deserts, grasslands, and evergreen forests are some biomes.

Many scientists say that the difference between a hill and a mountain is that a mountain has at least two zones of climate and plant life, or two biomes, at different elevations. That usually means a mountain rises at least 2,000 feet (610 m) above the surrounding land. In most parts of the world, a mountain must be that tall to have two life zones. Many mountains are much taller and have more life zones.

The number of life zones, or biomes, varies between mountain ranges. However, four basic zones have been identified. Starting at the bottom

These mountains are part of the Teton Mountain Range, in Wyoming, which is part of the Rocky Mountains.

Some of the mountains in the Himalaya are so tall that no animals or plants live in these cold, snowy mountaintops.

of a mountain and ascending, the four zones are foothills, montane, subalpine, and alpine zones. Very tall mountains may have a higher zone where almost nothing lives or grows.

Climate of Mountain Biomes

Mountain biomes get colder as the elevation rises. As a general rule, the temperature drops about 18° F (10° C) with each 3,281-foot (1,000 m) increase in elevation. Exact temperatures differ between mountain ranges. The climate in very tall ranges may vary from tropical at the bottom to arctic at the top.

Rainfall also varies between mountain ranges. Mountains may be wetter on one side than the other. Warm, moist air rising up a mountainside

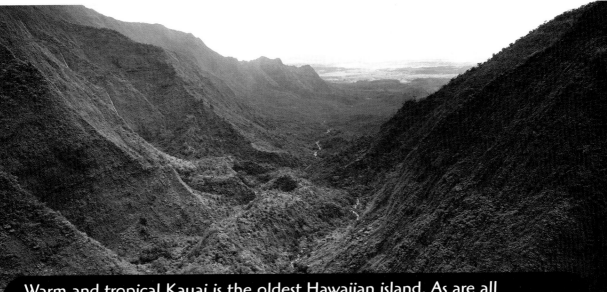

Warm and tropical Kauai is the oldest Hawaiian island. As are all Hawaiian Islands, Kauai is actually the top of an underwater mountain.

The climate at the base of India's Shivling Peak is warm and wet, but the weather at the peak is cold and dry.

cools and forms clouds, which produce rain or snow. By the time the clouds reach the mountaintop, their moisture is gone. This creates a rain shadow, an area on the other side that receives little rain.

Why does climate differ so much between mountain ranges? Location plays an important part.

Where in the World Are Mountains?

Mountains cover about 20 percent of Earth's surface and appear in all Earth's climate zones. A mountain may stand alone or with other mountains. Mountain groups may be small or large. They occur on all continents and many islands. They also exist on ocean bottoms. In fact, many islands are the tops of underwater mountains!

North America has three major mountain systems. The Appalachian Mountains extend about 1,500 miles (2,415 km), from Alabama to southern Canada. The Rocky Mountains stretch about 3,300 miles (5,311 km), from New Mexico through Canada to Alaska. The Pacific Mountain System runs about 2,500 miles (4,025 km), from southern California through Canada to Alaska.

South America has the Andes Mountains, which are the world's longest continuous chain of mountains on land. They stretch about 4,500 miles (7,242 km) along the continent's west coast.

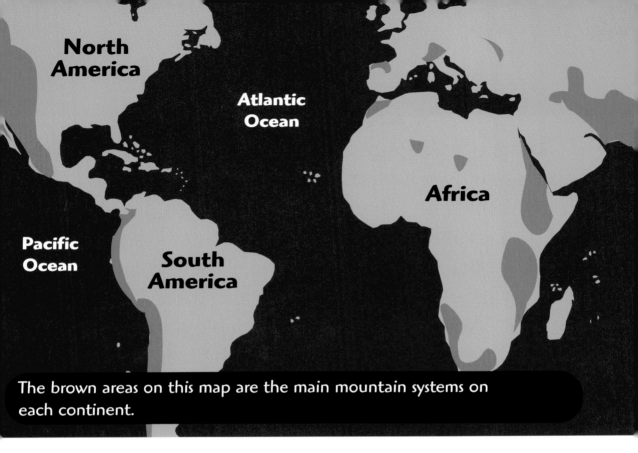

The brown areas on this map are the main mountain systems on each continent.

The Tethyan Mountain System, which is not continuous, runs about 6,850 miles (11,024 km), from northern Africa through Europe to Asia. This mountain system includes the Atlas Mountains in Africa, the Alps in Europe, and the Himalaya in Asia.

Denali, or Mount McKinley, in Alaska, is North America's tallest mountain at 20,320 feet (6,194 m). It is part of the Alaska Range.

Mountain Plants

Different plants grow in different mountain ranges and systems. The mountains' location and each region's climate affect the plant species growing there. Elevation also affects the plants. Generally, forests occupy the lower zones. The tree species change as elevation increases, and trees become smaller. Wind and cold may produce very short, twisted trees called krummholz. The tree line is the point beyond which trees cannot grow. Above the tree line is the alpine zone, with grasses, very low shrubs, and sturdy flowers. Let's look more closely at a couple of very different mountain ranges.

Many plant species grow in the northern, or tropical, part of the Andes Mountains. Tropical forests occupy the lower slopes. Next are cloud forests, which have a wide variety of trees, including palms. Polylepis forests also appear here. Above

Ferns like this one grow in tropical forests on the lower slopes of the Andes and other mountains found in tropical areas.

13

the forests are grasslands and the alpine zone. Mosses, grasses, and sedges grow here. At the highest elevations, nothing grows.

Europe's Alps have deciduous forests on the lower slopes. Here, as well as in the Andes, people have destroyed much of the forests to create farmland. Above the deciduous forests are short pine trees. Next come krummholz and short shrubs. Above them is the alpine meadow. Flowering plants have been recorded at elevations above 13,120 feet (4,000 m). Nothing grows at the highest elevations.

That's a Lot of Plants!

Scientists think the tropical Andes have 30,000 to 35,000 plant species. That is about 10 percent of all the plant species in the world! No other place has so many plant species.

This alpine meadow grows on Ring Mountain in Canada.

Mountain Animals

Many animal species live in the mountains. As with plants, the mountains' location and the region's climate affect which animal species live there. Climates at different elevations also have an effect, although some animal species wander between zones.

Reptiles, amphibians, and fish occupy only the warmer lower levels. Birds, insects, and mammals live in all the climate zones. Mammals at the lower levels include mice, chipmunks, coyotes, moose, rhinoceroses, elephants, leopards, and tigers. Bears, deer, elk, hares, mountain lions, wolves, foxes, squirrels, and monkeys live at the higher levels. Mountain goats and sheep, elk, leopards, bears, and mountain hares occupy the alpine zone. Let's look again at the Andes and Alps to learn about some of their animals.

Mountain lions live in many of North America's alpine forests. These big cats can weigh as much as 180 pounds (82 kg).

Many fish, reptile, and amphibian species live in the lower Andes. The forests are home to butterflies, frogs, lizards, mice, rats, bears, deer, monkeys, weasels, and many birds, including parrots, Andean condors, and hummingbirds. Llamas and two relatives, alpacas and vicuñas, live in the alpine zone. Chinchillas also make their homes there.

Many amphibians, reptiles, fish, birds, and butterflies live in the lower Alps. Owls, deer, marmots, lynxes, wolves, bears, and chamois live in the forest. Chamois and marmots are also found in the alpine zone, along with eagles, mountain hares, and goats called ibexes.

The Andes Are Humming

The Andes have more hummingbird species than any other place. They also have the world's largest hummingbird. The giant hummingbird is about 8 inches (20 cm) long. That is about twice as long as hummingbirds in North America.

The chamois is built perfectly to live high on the rocky mountains of the Alps in Italy and other places.

The Rocky Mountains

The Rocky Mountains are North America's largest mountain system. Several ranges, including the Southern, Middle, and Northern Rockies, make up the system.

The Rockies have four noticeable seasons. Winter has heavy snowfall, great winds, and blizzard conditions. Spring days can change from warm to cold. A sunny summer day can turn to thunderstorms. Fall is cool and windy.

The foothills have sagebrush, deciduous trees, pines, spruce, and other evergreens. The montane zone has pines, spruce, other evergreens, and

That's Heavy!

Male bighorn sheep fight each other with their large curved horns. The horns can weigh up to 30 pounds (14 kg). That is more than the weight of all their bones put together!

The highest peak in the Rocky Mountain system is Mount Elbert, which rises to 14,440 feet (4,401 m) above sea level.

Bighorn sheep make their home in the alpine meadows, slopes, and foothills of the Rocky Mountains.

grasses. Pines, cedars, and spruce occupy the subalpine zone. As trees approach the tree line, they grow shorter and finally become krummholz. Grasses, sedges, clovers, low shrubs, flowers, and mushrooms grow in the alpine zone. Nothing grows at the highest elevations.

Chipmunks, coyotes, buffalo, moose, frogs, turtles, and bluebirds live in the foothills. Bears, elk, hares, wolves, jays, and owls occupy the montane and subalpine zones. In summer, elk and deer visit the alpine zone, where they join snowshoe hares, mountain goats, and bighorn sheep.

The Himalaya

The Himalaya are the world's highest mountain system and have the world's tallest mountain, Mount Everest. There are only two seasons: a long, very cold winter and a short, cool summer.

What Is in a Name?

The name "Himalaya" comes from Sanskrit, the ancient language of India. Hima means "snow," and alaya means "house." So Himalaya, then, means "house of snow."

Yaks, like this one, live on hills and mountains. Their thick fur helps keep them warm in the cold areas they call home.

Mushrooms, grasslands, tropical deciduous forests, and evergreens grow in the foothills. The montane zone has temperate deciduous and evergreen forests. More plant species grow in the subalpine zone's evergreen forests than anywhere else. However, people have destroyed much of the forests. In the lower alpine zone, evergreen forests give way to shrubs, grasslands, and meadows. Above this are rocky, snow-covered peaks where nothing grows.

Reptiles, amphibians, and fish live in the lower Himalaya. Insects and birds occupy all zones except the snow-covered peaks. The foothills have tigers, leopards, elephants, rhinoceroses, water buffalo, deer, red pandas, and monkeys. Bears, weasels, squirrels, monkeys, and goatlike animals called tahrs live in the montane zone. Bears, weasels, tahrs, and snow leopards occupy the subalpine and alpine zones. Mountain goats, blue sheep, deer, and yaks, a type of ox, live in the alpine zone.

The red panda lives in the foothills of the Himalaya, where bamboo is plentiful. The red panda lives almost entirely on bamboo.

People of the Himalaya

Few people can live in the high mountains, but Sherpas have lived in the Himalaya for centuries. They occupy small villages, raise yaks, and grow potatoes. Yaks provide milk, butter, cheese, wool for clothes, leather for shoes, and dung for fuel. Potatoes form the basis of the Sherpas' diet. They drink mostly tea.

High elevations have thin air, with less oxygen than air at lower elevations. Sherpas function in this thin air much better than other people. Scientists are not sure why. Some think Sherpas have greater lung volume than other people. Others think their blood can carry more oxygen. Whatever the reason, it allows Sherpas to live where few people dare to go.

Outstanding Mountain Climbers

Sherpas are famous as guides for expeditions trying to climb Mount Everest. Sherpa guide Tenzing Norgay was one of the first two men to reach the top of Mount Everest.

This village in Nepal sits on the rock mountainside of the Himalaya.

Protecting Mountain Biomes

   Today, mountain biomes are at risk. Dangers include the increasing human population, people destroying forests, hunting, farm animals competing with wild animals for food, farm animals spreading illnesses to wild animals, people harvesting too many wild plants for natural medicines, pollution, and global warming.

   People are beginning to work on protecting mountain biomes. They are creating parks to preserve the biomes. They are trying to keep too many people from crowding into mountain regions. They are moving farm animals away from areas needed by wild animals. They are trying to help local people find ways to earn money that will not put mountain biomes in danger. If we all work together, we may be able to keep mountain biomes safe.

Deforestation, or cutting down trees, is one of the problems facing the mountain biomes.

Mountain Facts and Figures

- The world's longest mountain system, the Mid-Atlantic Ridge, is over 10,000 miles (16,100 km) long along the Atlantic Ocean bottom.

- Alpine wind speeds can exceed 150 miles per hour (241 km/h).

- Some alpine plants have red coloring that turns sunlight into heat.

- Butterflies might not seem sturdy, but they can live in alpine zones.

- The first potatoes grew in the Andes Mountains.

- A tree rat as big as a cat lives in forests of the Andes Mountains.

- Rocky Mountain National Park's oldest rocks are 1.7 billion years old.

- More than 5,000 plant species grow in the Rocky Mountains.

- Mountains affect climate. The Himalaya keep arctic winds out of India.

- Himalayan forests and forest animals are disappearing. One-fourth of the species found only in the Himalaya could vanish by 2100.

Glossary

chinchillas (chin-CHIH-luz) Animals related to squirrels that have soft gray fur.

cloud forests (KLOWD FOHR-ests) Very wet forests in tropical mountains that are often covered in clouds.

deciduous (deh-SIH-joo-us) Having leaves that fall off every year.

mammals (MA-mulz) Warm-blooded animals that have a backbone and hair, breathe air, and feed milk to their young.

marmots (MAHR-muts) Stout-bodied animals related to squirrels. Marmots have a short tail and small ears, and live underground.

mountain ranges (MOWN-tun RAYN-jez) Series of mountains. Two or more mountain ranges together form a mountain system.

polylepis (pah-lee-LEH-puhs) Any of several evergreen species related to roses.

species (SPEE-sheez) A single kind of living thing. All people are one species.

temperate (TEM-puh-rit) Not too hot or too cold.

temperature (TEM-pur-cher) How hot or cold something is.

tropical (TRAH-puh-kul) Having to do with or similar to conditions in the warm parts of Earth that are near the equator, the line around the center of Earth.

Index

Web Sites

Due to the changing nature of Internet links, PowerKids Press has
developed an online list of Web sites related to the subject of this book.
This site is updated regularly. Please use this link to access the list:
www.powerkidslinks.com/whab/mountain/